MIRACLE IN JERUSALEM

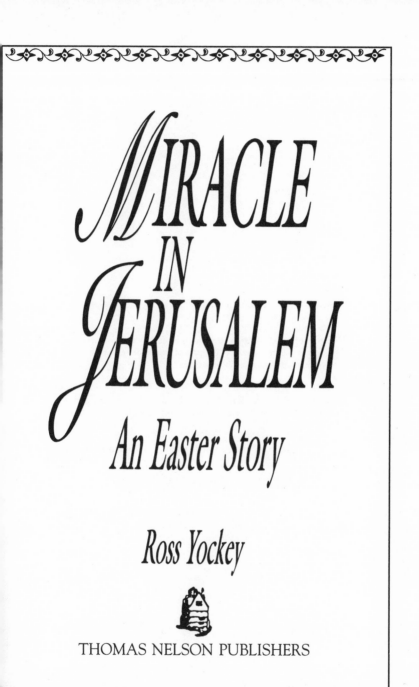

MIRACLE IN JERUSALEM

An Easter Story

Ross Yockey

THOMAS NELSON PUBLISHERS

Published in Nashville, Tennessee, by Thomas Nelson, Inc., and
distributed in Canada by Lawson Falle, Ltd., Cambridge, Ontario.

Library of Congress Cataloging-in-Publication Data

Yockey, Ross.
    Miracle in Jerusalem : an Easter story / Ross Yockey.
        p.   cm.
    ISBN 0-8407-7682-9
    1. Jesus Christ—Fiction.   2. Bible.   N.T.—History of Biblical
events—Fiction.   I. Title.
PS3575.O27M5   1991
813'.54—dc20   91-30517
                                                                    CIP

Printed in the United States of America

        1   2   3   4   5   6   7   -   96   95   94   93   92   91

FOREWORD

*iracle in Jerusalem* plunges us into those turbulent events of Christ's final week in Jerusalem, the time Christians observe now as Holy Week. We are eyewitnesses to Palm Sunday, the Cleansing of the Temple, the Last Supper, Good Friday, and the Resurrection. However, our eyes are not those of the main characters in this world-shaking drama. Instead we see through the eyes of children who are swept up in events that would change the course of history. These are the children who would become the fathers of the Church we know today.

Miracle in Jerusalem is the Gospel proclaimed in an exciting way. The story recreates the electrifying power that transforms men and women and boys and girls when they find that God's love has overshadowed their lives and forever changed them. Here is a story that becomes more alive with each telling. It is meant to be seen, touched, then "passed on down" to someone else. The real miracle takes place in our hearts when we are drawn into understanding the profound simplicity of God's love, when we discover that love in a simple smile or in a moment of shared laughter.

Miracle in Jerusalem is about how teaching and being taught are one and the same. It gently urges us to have faith enough to try—to try for miracles of our own. And, just in case we are adults who have our heads in the cloud cover of modern life, it beckons us back to our own childhood, where the best miracles have always been.

Jay Alan Hobbs
Asheboro, 1989

CONTENTS

1. Somebody's Coming   13
2. The Big Parade   27
3. Miracles?   47
4. The Money Changers   73
5. The Rich Man's Son   87
6. Seder News   103
7. Sorrowful Days   125
8. At the Tomb   137

POEMS

Miracles   24
Halleloo   44
Pass It on Down   70
Little Children Come to Me   84
Teachers   100
Rachel's Wish   122
Gather Flowers   134

*G*o back a thousand years ago. Now go back yet a thousand years more to a faraway time of chariots and chains, of camel hide sandals and cloaks that become blankets at night.

To some who live in this time, in the little-big hill city of Jerusalem, this is an almost ordinary Sunday of an ordinary week in a very ordinary year. To some it is a time of baking bread and breaking bread, of tending flocks and tending shops. To some it is a time of playing roughhouse games with good friends in the dust of clamorous, cramped streets till nightfall. To others, this is a time of miracles.

It is a true thing about miracles, yet a strange thing still, that when they happen they always begin in perfectly ordinary ways. A miracle can have its birth in a ho-hum little thing you'd not be tempted to notice. Say, in a mother's prayer as she sweeps the floor with a stubby straw broom. Say, in the small, squeaky voice of a skinned-kneed little girl . . .

SOMEBODY'S COMING

*S*omebody's coming!"

It was Sarah, the youngest of the orphans, who burst in first. Rachel looked up from the oven, where she was checking on the bread, to shush her. It made no difference. Sarah kept right on twittering, just like a nervous little hoopoe bird.

Like most children, Sarah understood that the shorter you are, the more noise you must make to be listened to. And Sarah was a rather short person.

"A parade!" she shouted, tugging on Rachel's sleeve. "You've got to come see. The whole city's buzzing."

"Calm down," said Rachel. She could see that her daughter, Elizabeth, was getting all worked up, just what Rachel was trying to avoid. Unfortunately, there was no avoiding it around rough-and-tumble Sarah.

"Really?" Elizabeth was saying, already sounding breathless. "A parade with marching and music?"

"And everything," panted Sarah, a bit out of breath herself. She had run all the way from the lamp-seller's shop three streets down, racing ahead of her friends. They were a gang of street orphans who had no real homes. Many people were kind and helpful to them, but none kinder or more helpful than Rachel. And no one was friendlier to them than Rachel's daughter. Sarah considered Elizabeth to be her best friend.

The door of Rachel's house was open to catch the morning breeze. So when the other orphans arrived, all huffing and puffing and talking at once, they tumbled in like puppies through a fence hole. Their names were Zebedee, Margaret, Simon, Samuel, and Rebecca. Sarah made six.

Zebedee, the oldest orphan, was also the loudest. "We don't know for sure about the parade part," he said, "but from what everybody says, this man who's coming is pretty big."

"You mean, like a giant?" Elizabeth's brown eyes opened wide.

Simon and Samuel, orphan brothers, slapped their faces in disbelief. They did everything in unison. "No," they groaned.

"Not *tall* big," said Simon.

"*Important* big," said Samuel.

"We've got to hurry if we don't want to miss it all," said Zebedee.

"Come with us," Sarah insisted. Her big pie-eyes darted from Rachel to Elizabeth and back again. "Come and see."

"Please, Mama?"

Rachel looked at her imploring daughter.

Elizabeth was almost the same age as Zebedee,
but she was a frail child, hardly bigger than
little Sarah. Elizabeth had been sick her whole
life, nearly twelve years.

As though reading Rachel's mind, Zebedee
said, "Don't worry, I'll look after Lizzy."

"It's a mother's job to worry, Zeb."

"But a parade!" Sarah got them started
again. Now the six orphans became a noisy
flock of hoopoe birds, twittering and chattering
all at once, with Elizabeth adding her song to
the others.

"Somebody's coming!"

"Drums and dulcimers!"

"Mama, please?"

"Camels and horses."

"Prob'ly soldiers marching, too."

"We've got to get running."

"*I* won't run, Mama. Honest."

Margaret and Rebecca were already out
the door, beckoning anxiously to the others.

As Simon and Samuel rushed to join
them, they bounced off the generous belly of a

SOMEBODY'S COMING

short, round man who was coming in at that very moment.

"Uncle Ezra!" cried Elizabeth. "Tell Mama it's okay. Please?"

"Well, er-ah, har-rumph," said the stout man, as though he meant great things by it.

Uncle Ezra was Rachel's favorite relative. He was, in fact, the only relative who would have anything to do with them since Rachel's divorce, more than ten years earlier. Since that awful time, Ezra had been like a father to both Rachel and Elizabeth.

Blocking the doorway now, Uncle Ezra rearranged his belly like a baker patting and pricking a big ball of dough. "What's the, ah, disturbance, hmm?"

Simon and Samuel pushed their way around Uncle Ezra, shouting at the others to get a move on.

"It's a parade," said Elizabeth.

"A *componderous* parade!" shouted Sarah. "Come on, Lizzy!"

Zebedee explained, "You see, Uncle Ezra,

it's this important somebody or other coming
to Jerusalem for Passover." (Now, even though
none of the orphans was related to Uncle Ezra,
he granted them all the privilege of calling him
Uncle.)

"Oh, now, yes! Yes, indeed." Uncle Ezra's
booming voice was the voice of authority. "Yes,
indeed. Mmm. You mean Yeshua, of course—
that strange Nazarene fellow. They say he'll be
here today. Yes. Well!"

Uncle Ezra was forever leaving thoughts
hanging like that, like robes left draped on the
backs of chairs. Rachel wished her uncle would
tidy up his sentences a bit.

"Well *what?*" she demanded.

"Well, uh, that is, yes. He *is* somebody
important. Quite important, I'd say. His name
is Yeshua. From Nazareth, in Galilee. Or did I
already mention that, hmm?"

"Oh, Mama," Elizabeth begged. "Can't I
go? *Please?*"

Zebedee put his lanky arm around
Elizabeth's shoulders and promised he would

look after her. With a sigh, Rachel gave in.
She knew excitement was hard on her
daughter's fragile heart. But she also knew that
without excitement there can be no childhood.
"Just be back by noon," she called as Elizabeth
dashed out the door. "And stay in the shade."

Quickly the children were gone.

Uncle Ezra chuckled, his woolly gray beard
rustling like wheat in the wind. "It's not easy
to say no, eh?"

Rachel let out a deep sigh and returned to
the oven. She felt tears well in her eyes. _No_
was the ugliest word she knew. Yet how often
she must repeat it these days, with Elizabeth's
condition growing worse and worse.

"No, Elizabeth, no toys from the market
this week."

"No, dear, we can't afford a new kid.
Maybe the Lord will send one."

"No, you can't play catch-me-catch-you
today. You were wheezing all night long."

"No, you may not go out until after your
nap."

And the worst of it was, Elizabeth could be so understanding. She knew her mother was doing the very best she could, and she accepted each refusal almost cheerfully. Yet the child was so brimming-over with life and joy that every no added a new link to the heavy chain they carried together.

"Why would the Lord make a child like that?" Rachel wondered aloud. "Surely not just to watch her waste away? Or is He so fond of hearing my prayers and my complaints?"

"Just the sort of question a woman would ask," growled Uncle Ezra. He had a very gruff way of comforting a person. "Would you rather the Lord had not sent her?"

Rachel decided to change the subject. "So who is this great visitor to Jerusalem?"

"Yeshua? Mmm, very difficult." Uncle Ezra was twisting his beard and rubbing his belly at the same time. "Hard to say. He's the great topic of conversation in the synagogues and the shops. Some people think, well, they think he's a king."

"A king?" Rachel asked in disbelief. She lowered her voice and looked about to make sure no one else was listening. Judea was not allowed to have a real king. Herod Antipas was the tetrarch, appointed by Rome. And Herod was a crafty Samaritan, beloved by very few in Jerusalem. Their Roman governor, Pontius Pilate, was quick to put down any uprising. And Pilate had plenty of Roman soldiers to help him.

"If your Yeshua's talking about crowns and thrones," Rachel said, "we're in for big trouble."

Harrumphing, Uncle Ezra called the matter a lot of gossip, around-the-well talk. "Why, there isn't a throne to be had in Jerusalem," he chuckled. "And besides, the intelligent folks say this Nazarene carpenter . . ."

"Carpenter?" Rachel cut him off, laughing. "Well, if he's a carpenter he can build his own throne."

$\mathscr{M}$IRACLES

$\mathscr{P}$erhaps they really did exist
Back in the distant mist of history.
They seem so once-upon-a-time,
Like fairy tales that rhyme, like mystery,
Mythology.

Would they be happening today,
If we knew how to pray for miracles?
If we should ask, might we receive?
But no one still believes in miracles,
In miracles.

We've never known
     that kind of faith.
We must be shown,
We are so wise, we have to see
With our own eyes.

They say that love begins to turn
To hope, when people yearn for miracles.
But love sometimes can make us grieve,
Forgetting to believe in miracles,
In miracles.

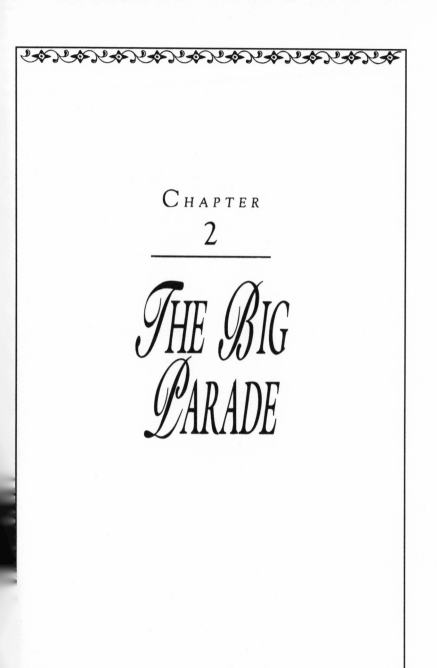

CHAPTER

2

THE BIG
PARADE

*W*hen you're an orphan, life is liable to have more downs than ups. When you're a short orphan, crowds are generally *downs*. Along the road outside the city gate people stood three- and four-deep, waiting for the big parade.

Sarah, short as she was noisy, did not care much for crowds. For one thing, crowds tended to pay very little attention to very little girls. For another, when the crowds were thick, Sarah often found herself pushed to the back where she couldn't see a thing. Having no father to heft her onto his shoulders, she would have been dependent on the older boys to lift her up. And Sarah would never ask a boy for help, not even if he was tending a camel that was standing on her toes.

Sarah was the sort who created her own ups in down situations, so instead of asking anyone for help she turned to the three other girls and said, "A tree. We need a tree."

Pulling Elizabeth, Margaret, and Rebecca along, Sarah worked her way around the edge of the murmuring, milling crowd. The townspeople were gathered just outside the northeastern gate to the city. This gate opened on a winding road that led up the Mount of Olives to the little town of Bethpage. Along the road there were lots of trees—olives, figs, palms, tamarisks, and cedars. But Sarah was looking for a particular tree.

"That one!" she decided at last, pointing to a young date palm. The tree was curved, bent low by strong winds before it had time

and girth enough to tell straight up from
sideways. It seemed to be making a deep bow,
like a servant bowing before a king.

Sarah's little bare feet kicked up a cloud of
dry sand and dust as she ran to the crooked
palm. Like a monkey, she scampered up the
curved trunk and made a place for herself. She
straddled the trunk just below the cluster of
dates and leaves at its crown. Margaret, tall
and spindly, was right behind her, followed by
stocky, strong-armed Rebecca. Elizabeth lagged
below, gazing up at her more athletic
companions.

Sarah yelled down, "It's a cinch, Lizzy.
You can do it."

Still Elizabeth held back.

"Her mama told her to take it easy," said
Margaret.

"Maybe she's afraid," offered Rebecca.

"Maybe you're stupid, Reba. Come on up,
Lizzy. You can see for a hundred miles."

Sometimes Sarah thought she understood
her friend Elizabeth better than anybody else

did. Being the smallest, she could sympathize with Lizzy, who was the weakest. Sarah also understood that missing one parent could be as hard on a kid as missing two.

There was a sadness in Lizzy's house that never seemed to go away, no matter how hard Lizzy tried to be cheerful. The sorrow came from her mother, Rachel. It was as though Rachel blamed herself for not having a husband, as though she even blamed herself for Lizzy's sickness. Sarah wondered whether Rachel had committed some awful sin to bring such sadness into their house.

They do say that when parents sin, God punishes their children, Sarah thought. *But if that's true, it's not fair. . . . And God's supposed to be fair.*

Satisfied with her own logic, she looked down at Lizzy trying to get a good hold on the tree trunk. Lizzy never blamed anybody for being sick. She didn't blame her mother, and she certainly didn't blame God. *Sometimes,* Sarah thought, *it is as though Lizzy does not even know she is sick.*

"Just pull with your fingers and push with your toes," she yelled down. "Your knees'll hold you to the tree."

Sarah watched Elizabeth grip the wrinkly bark with her arms and legs. Most children could climb tall palms that stretched straight up into the sky. Surely even Lizzy could manage this old leaning tree.

Sarah felt a powerful urge in her friend to be normal, to be just like other children. *Maybe Lizzy kind of owes it to her mother to be like the rest of us,* Sarah thought, *even though she has to disobey her mother to do it.* Surely Rachel would not object to Lizzy climbing this one little tree. Surely not.

Sarah grinned from her perch. "See, I told you. It's a cinch." But Sarah could not help noticing how Elizabeth stopped to catch her breath only a few feet above the ground.

"Where's Zeb?" Elizabeth panted. "He can't see me, can he? He's supposed to be taking care of me."

MIRACLE IN JERUSALEM

"Uh-uh," Margaret answered, pointing back toward the gate. "The boys are way back there in the crowd. Hurry up, Liz."

As she waited for Elizabeth to join them, Sarah nudged Rebecca. Just below them stood a Roman soldier. The sunlight splashed against his helmet and shimmered from the handle of his short sword. The soldier's leather jerkin was soaked with sweat.

Hebrew children were taught at an early age to despise all Romans. After all, didn't Romans hate Jews?

Sarah yanked a hard, orange-colored date from the tree and passed it to Rebecca. "Dare you," she whispered.

Rebecca grinned, crinkling her freckled nose, and took aim. *Bonk!* The date bounced off the gleaming helmet and left a little smudge.

Startled, the man jerked his head first this way, then that. When at last he looked up, the girls were pointing into the distance, pretending they didn't know the soldier was

THE BIG PARADE

standing below them. But, if the Roman was
listening at all, he must have heard a high-
pitched giggle coming from above.

Delighted with the prank, Sarah waited
until the soldier glanced away to risk a
backward glance down the trunk. Elizabeth had
almost made it! She was barely inches from the
curve where the trunk became a fine bench for
parade watching. Once again, however,
Elizabeth was taking a break to catch her
breath.

"Come on, Lizzy." Margaret urged. Nearest
to Elizabeth, she offered a hand. "Up you go."

Sarah watched as Elizabeth reached out,
almost touching Margaret's long fingers.

Then Lizzy quivered and began to lose
her balance.

"Aaa!" screamed Elizabeth.

"Uh-oh," said Rebecca.

"Hang on, Lizzy," cried Sarah. "Hang on."

But it was too late. Elizabeth slid around
the palm trunk as though it were greased with
olive oil. She tried to grip it with her knees

and forearms, but they simply were not strong enough. Sarah watched in horror as the trunk slipped out of Lizzy's grasp and she plunged head first toward the rocky earth.

Just at that moment, in the nick of time, the Roman soldier ran up to catch Elizabeth in midair. She landed in his big, burly arms like a bird in a nest.

From her perch, Sarah heard the foreigner growling those *uss*-ing and *ump*-ing sounds Romans used for words. Unable to make out a thing the soldier was saying, Lizzy just whimpered. Her eyes were wide and brimming with tears.

"I'm coming," Sarah shouted. She shut her eyes and let go.

She hit the ground with a thud, tearing her knee on a rock. But in her fear for Lizzy's safety, Sarah hardly noticed her own pain. The wiry little girl bounced to her feet and began tugging on the soldier's arms, demanding that he set her friend down. Of course, the soldier understood not a word of Sarah's abuse.

Somehow, despite interference from Sarah, the Roman got Elizabeth safely on the ground. She appeared more terrified and weakened than injured, though her hands were scratched and bloody.

Sarah, who was by and large the cause of Elizabeth's predicament, now determined that she must be the rescuer. "The sun!" she exclaimed. "We've got to get you some shade quick."

Sarah ran to a nearby palmetto, a sort of stubby palm bush without much of a trunk. She yanked and twisted at its big leaves, trying to pull them loose. With those leaves she could bring Lizzy some shade, some cooling breeze. But it was no use. The leaves would not come off.

All at once Sarah felt the soldier standing beside her. With a shock, she saw his sword drawn and raised high above his head. The soldier's brow was furrowed deep with determination.

Oh, no! Sarah thought. *He knows we threw*

the date at him. He's going to kill me!

Swooosh!

The short steel blade cut the air, and four palmetto leaves fell onto the sand. Sarah shook her head to make sure it was still attached to her neck, then grinned sheepishly at the soldier. *So he just wants to help*, she thought. *A big Roman helping a little Jewish girl!*

Feeling slightly guilty, Sarah quickly gathered up the leaves and ran to Elizabeth, who by now was sitting up and feeling just fine.

Sarah made an enormous fan of the palm leaves and waved them over her friend's head. "I'm all right now," Elizabeth assured her. She held up her hands to protect her face from the swatting of the huge leaves. "I'll be okay, really."

But Sarah went right on fanning and swatting.

Now the murmur of the crowd grew noticeably louder. "They're coming," shouted Margaret and Rebecca from their perch in the palm tree. "We can see them."

At last! Sarah thought, all at once forgetting her nursemaid role. *It must be the man from Galilee!* "Here comes the parade!" she shouted.

The noise of the crowd became a roar as men and women began to point and shout and wave their arms.

"Let's go," Sarah said, pulling Lizzy to her feet.

"No more trees," Elizabeth insisted.

"All right. But we came to see a parade, and we are going to *see* it."

Sarah strode toward the road, pushing forward with her palmetto fan, parting the crowd like Moses parting the Red Sea. Elizabeth did her best to keep up. Soon the two girls were standing at the edge of the roadway, watching a dusty band of men approach on foot. Only one of the men, who seemed to be the leader, was riding.

"A *donkey?*"

Sarah could not believe her eyes. She

stepped out into the road and put her hands on her slim hips. "This was supposed to be a big parade!" she exclaimed. "Elephants, camels, musicians, acrobats! All we get is a dumb _donkey?_"

"Hush," said Elizabeth, pulling her to the side of the road. "Just watch. Listen."

Sarah was disappointed, and she started to give Lizzy a piece of her mind. Then she became aware of a strange look on her friend's face, a look Sarah had never seen. The look stopped Sarah's wagging tongue and, almost magically, the crowd fell still at the same moment.

Silence swept over them like a calming wave. Here arose a cry, there a shout of welcome, but Sarah felt a curious kind of peace as the little band of men drew near. Lizzy, on the other hand, seemed tense, nervous, as though something unusual were about to happen.

"It isn't right," Elizabeth said in a clipped and determined whisper. "He's getting all dusty.

There should be carpets spread over this road."

"Someone should have got him a horse," said Sarah. "A big white one with lots of gold braid and a red bridle. Somebody should have planned this better."

"We can't give him a horse," said Elizabeth, speaking louder in that same serious, urgent voice. She snatched the palm leaves from Sarah's hands. "But we *can* give him a carpet."

Sarah watched, astonished, as her friend ran down the road toward the oncoming procession. What had come over her? All of a sudden Elizabeth was spreading the palms across the road, right in the little donkey's path.

The donkey stopped, as if wondering what it should do next. Elizabeth went down on her knees.

The man on the donkey smiled and reached out to touch Elizabeth's head. Sarah watched as he lifted Lizzy's chin to look deeply into her eyes.

As the man on the donkey motioned for

Elizabeth to rise, someone in the crowd
shouted, "A carpet!"

"Yes," said another voice. "Make a carpet
for the Master."

From everywhere came bundles of palm
leaves and olive branches carried by men,
women, and children of all ages. The road
became a carpet of green from where Elizabeth
stood all the way to the city gates.

People took off their scarves and kerchiefs
to wave them in the air. Others waved
branches like banners.

Near the bent palm where her two friends
sat, Sarah saw a group of old men laughing and
dancing in a circle.

Now, thought Sarah, *now it's starting to
look like a parade!*

She watched in amazement as even the
big Roman pushed through the crush of
townspeople to get a better look at the man on
the donkey.

*Uncle Ezra was sure right when he said this
man was somebody important.*

Still . . .

Still . . . Sarah said to herself, as the man they called the Master moved past her, *if you ask me, they should have had him riding on a big white horse.*

HALLELOO

They should have had a carpet,
Yes, they should have rolled it out,
'Cause Jerusalem was jumping.
There is just no doubt
That they should have had some banners,
With an honor guard, of course,
And they should have had him riding
      On a big white horse.

      Hallelujah, hallelujah!
      Didn't know it would be you.
      Hallelujah, hallelujah, *Halleloo!*

They should have tooted trumpets
And they should have beat the drums,
For it isn't every Sunday
Someone special comes.

Yes, they should have made some music,
But the orchestra was out,
So the people raised their voices
    In a joyful shout!

    Hallelujah, hallelujah!
    Didn't know it would be you.
    Hallelujah, hallelujah, *Halleloo!*

They hailed him with their kerchiefs,
Oh, they lifted up their arms,
Then they ran to cut the branches
From the roadside palms.
Soon the leaves became their banners
And the air got green and sweet.
Then they laid them like a carpet
    For the dusty street.

    Hallelujah, hallelujah!
    Didn't know it would be you.
    Hallelujah, hallelujah, *Halleloo!*

Oh, they should have had him riding
    On a big, white horse.

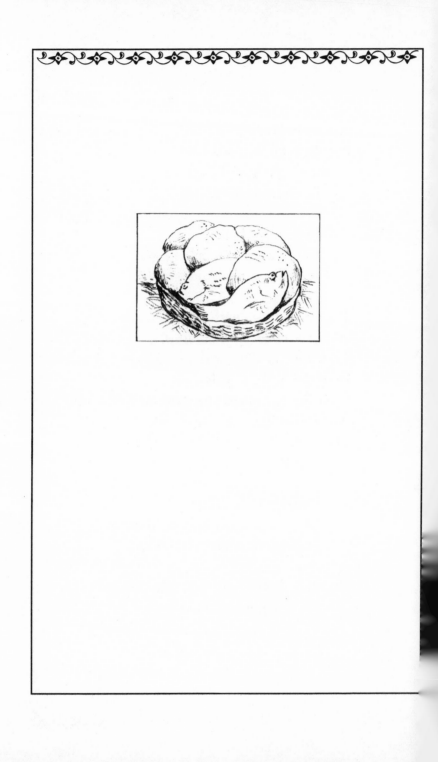

CHAPTER

3

MIRACLES?

On Monday Elizabeth slept late. Nothing could wake her. She even slept through the noise of the nanny goat baaing to be milked in her ground floor stall.

Rachel could not recall seeing her daughter so exhausted. The excitement of the previous day had been too much for the child. She seemed to be getting worse and worse. *Her sickness must be a curse on me*, Rachel thought, *just as all the gossips say. The mother sins; the daughter is punished.*

Rachel stood in the doorway, looking out.
Their house was not tall, only two stories. Yet,
because of the way the narrow street curved
and because the city was built on a hilltop, if
you leaned against the door frame just so, you
could see over the city walls and into the
valley beyond.

It was a narrow view, but it seemed to go
on forever, widening as a trickle of water
spreads itself out upon the sand. The rolling
hills with their ragged scallops of green gave
way to the barren lands, sculpted into shifting
darks and lights by the sun. Ocher flames of
sunlight flicked yellow tongues, leaving umber
ashes along the high ridges. In the far distance
were ghosts of mountains, melted from the
molten sky.

As she stood there, plaiting her knee-
length hair into a thick brown braid, Rachel
wished she could follow the path her eyes made
from the narrow doorway into the ever-
widening world. The change would be so good
for her. It would be so good for Elizabeth.

Life is not turning out the way it should have,
thought Rachel. *One day a young woman
prepares the meals for her husband. One day she
gossips with other young wives at the well, hears
their hopes for the child growing inside her. One
day she laughs at her husband's old jokes after the
evening prayers, and they sit together on the roof,
close and caring under the star-sprinkled sky.*

*The next day life is ruined by scandal and
divorce. The next day her Zealot husband hears a
story she thought long forgotten.*

"The Roman soldier," her husband cries. *"It
was you!"*

*A young girl's careless mistake and an
unforgiving God.*

"I was so young," she weeps *(knowing this is
no excuse: even children learn the Law).* *"I didn't
understand."*

*"You took him alone into your father's
house,"* shouts the angry husband, throwing her to
the floor.

"The mob would have killed him."

"They should have killed him. You should

have let them kill him. Instead . . ." The
husband's words are too shameful to be spoken.

*"Nothing happened," she weeps, lying
facedown on the hard floor. "I only gave him a
hiding place."*

*"Alone with him in your father's house. A
foreigner. A Roman!" The word curls from his
lips like the snarl of a dog. "You know the Law.
And now the Law says I can divorce you. My
honor demands it."*

*How simple a solution for the husband. Put
his wife away. No stain of the sin on his garment.
How hard on the wife. Branded with double guilt.
First the mistake, then the divorce.*

*And the guilt is trebled when she bears a
child. The child is sickly, sure proof of the Lord's
righteous anger.*

*Have as little as possible to do with a woman
like that. Pity her, but keep your distance. Pretend
not to see her at the well. . . .*

Uncle Ezra tumbled in, bursting with news
and popping the bubble of Rachel's melancholy
thoughts. He nearly bowled her over as he

pushed his way through the door. Still, the old
man made Rachel smile. Uncle Ezra was her
staff now, the one person in Jerusalem she
could depend upon. He cared for her and
Elizabeth, truly cared, even if his love was
touched with pity.

"Is . . . is it true?" Ezra demanded.
"Well? Well?" At the sight of Lizzy still on her
sleeping mat beneath the window he lowered
his voice. "Isss it t-t-true?"

"No need to whisper," Rachel said. "I
believe she'll sleep through anything this
morning. Is what true?"

"This is most unusual," Uncle Ezra puffed,
looking down at the sleeping girl, "most, ah,
ex-ex-extraordinary."

Rachel thought he meant the way
Elizabeth sprawled across the mat with one foot
tucked under the opposite knee. But that was
not the extraordinary thing her uncle was
talking about.

"They say he touched our Lizzy yesterday,
Rachel. Four people told me about it this

morning. We could have some sort of miracle in store. There's no telling."

"Slow down, Uncle Ezra," said Rachel. "Who touched Elizabeth?"

"Yeshua. They say he reached out his hand and laid it on her head as he entered the city."

"It's true." The small voice belonged to Sarah. She was standing on the roof of the stable, peeping in the window over Lizzy's bed. "He did touch her," said Sarah, "right on the head. I saw it with my own eyes."

Uncle Ezra tugged at his beard, patted his tummy, paced, and muttered.

Now that, Sarah thought, watching the old man do all four of his tics at once, _is extraordinary_.

"Hmmph, er, umm, well," he said.

Rachel declared that she saw no particular significance in a stranger touching her child in passing. Elizabeth was a pretty, polite girl. Grownups often gave her a pat of approval, even when they knew she

was Rachel's daughter.

"But this is no ordinary, ah, grownup," said Uncle Ezra. "They claim he raises people from the dead. Makes the deaf walk."

"He makes the deaf *hear*," Sarah corrected. Now she was sitting on the window sill, her battered sandals swinging and scraping against the wall, just over the head of the sleeping Elizabeth. There was a bloodstained rag bandaging Sarah's thin left knee, a badge of yesterday's adventure.

"Yes, and the lame walk," Uncle Ezra went on.

"A carpenter from Nazareth?" Rachel said. "And you *believe* it?"

"Well," replied Uncle Ezra, lost in his own thoughts, "Nazareth is a long way off, but I imagine there must be carpenters there."

Sarah giggled.

"Uncle Ezra!" Rachel was growing exasperated. "The city is full of magicians these days. They claim to cure the sick. They claim to raise the dead. They pull doves from their sleeves and people believe them."

"This one is different," said Uncle Ezra.
"The priests, the Sadducees, the Pharisees,
they're all talking about him. They're all a bit
worried."

Uncle Ezra went on to report what was
being whispered around town concerning the
popular newcomer. Some people were talking
about Yeshua drumming up an army of
rebels. They were talking about *a revolt against
Rome.*

Rachel did not like what she was hearing.
"Do you think he's a revolutionary?" she asked.
"Have you heard him speak?"

"Not yet," Uncle Ezra said, "but I, uh,
well, I certainly intend to."

There was a noise at the door, a clank of
metal. Rachel looked up to see the three
orphans, Zebedee, Simon, and Samuel, along
with another boy and—she rose, suddenly
frightened—a Roman soldier!

"Don't be scared," said Zebedee.
"There's no problem."

It certainly seemed like a problem to
Rachel. What was a Roman soldier doing at
her house? And wearing his sword! The last
time a Roman entered her house he had
brought ruin on her.

"Filia tua," the soldier said in a deep, calm
voice. "Bene est?"

Now the other stranger spoke up. He
was a short, tough-looking boy with very
dark skin, a round face, and deep, dark eyes.
The pattern of cloth in his shirt set him apart
as a stranger, a Jew who did not live in
Jerusalem. "He wants to know about your
daughter," the boy said, "if she's okay."

Rachel leaned against the table. Her knees
felt weak. She nodded at the Roman, looking
for the first time into his eyes. She saw nothing
but trouble there.

"Look here," said Uncle Ezra, taking
charge. (Rachel said a silent prayer of thanks
for Uncle Ezra.) He stepped over to the mat
under the window and patted Elizabeth's
head. "Girl sleeping. Girl fine."

"Dormit," said the boy to the soldier.

The Roman stepped into the room. He was so tall and muscular that the house seemed to shrink around him. Rachel backed away from him, in fear, but when the soldier stepped toward the window, Rachel moved quickly to place herself between him and her daughter. She felt Uncle Ezra's soft hand on her arm.

"He means, uh, means no harm, my dear." Rachel understood somehow that Uncle Ezra was right. She stepped aside and let the Roman pass. There was a smell of sweat and battle about him, the smell of death.

The soldier strode over to the mat and knelt on one knee, looking down at Elizabeth. He lifted her hands and inspected the cuts caused by the rough bark of the date palm. Then he spotted the girl seated in the window. (Sarah gave him a little wag of her fingers, hoping no one else would notice. There were any number of ways she could get into trouble in this situation.)

The square-jawed soldier looked down at

Elizabeth and brushed her hair with his
fingertips. Rachel looked on in awed silence.
She had observed it before, this special gift of
her daughter's. It gave her the power to break
down the barriers between people, to bring
laughter into a somber room. But . . . *a
Roman!*

The soldier whispered something into
Elizabeth's ear, smiled, and rose, putting his
finger to his lips in a sign of quiet. The
Roman raised his hand and nodded to Sarah.
Then, ducking through the door, he was
gone.

At first Rachel could only close her eyes
and breathe deeply. Slowly she recovered from
her fear and shock and demanded, "What's
going on?"

She looked from one orphan to the next.
Her gaze fell at last on Sarah. *This child*, Rachel
decided, *has a great deal more information than
she is giving out.* "What was that all about?
Sarah, talk!"

Sarah swung her legs, carefully letting one

sandal slip off her foot and fall on Elizabeth's
ear. She hoped her friend would wake up and
help her out of this unpleasant predicament.
But Lizzy slept on. Sarah would have to face
the music alone.

Mustering her courage, she dropped from
her perch and shuffled with one bare foot
toward Rachel. *The important thing*, she
instructed herself, *is not to begin this story at the
beginning*.

In short sentences with long pauses, Sarah
told Rachel and the others how the Roman
soldier had broken Lizzy's fall from the tree,
how he had cut the palm branches, how he
had followed Lizzy into the crowd to place
branches on the roadway. Of course Sarah was
careful to leave out her own parts in the story
—except for when she bravely fanned Elizabeth
with the palms to keep her cool.

"Well, then," said Uncle Ezra, "the fellow
was simply concerned for her condition. Quite,
uh, mannerly, for a Roman."

"*Mannerly* is hardly the word, Uncle Ezra.

Romans do not come to the rescue of Jews. They do not enter the homes of Jews. They despise us as much as we are supposed to despise them."

Rachel turned to confront the children by the door. "Zebedee . . ." she began, about to ask why he had allowed Elizabeth to climb a tree. But Zeb knew what was coming, so he quickly cut her off.

"Correct," he said. "I have forgotten to introduce our friend Lemuel. He's from Capernaum. And he speaks Latin, as you may have noticed."

"Only a little," said Lemuel.

"But wait till you hear his story," said Zebedee.

"It's incredible!" said Samuel and Simon, in unison, as though they had rehearsed it.

Uncle Ezra suggested they go downstairs, into the courtyard, so as not to disturb Elizabeth. But just then Elizabeth stirred.

"If there's a story to be heard, I want to hear it," she said.

In the end, they all descended the ladder to the ground-floor courtyard. Rachel was too caught up in her puzzling thoughts to protest the disturbance of Lizzy's rest. The Roman and the man from Galilee—what had they to do with her daughter? There must be a meaning in all this.

Rachel wished she could ask her grandmother who used to be so good with meanings, but her grandmother was dead. She would have to discover this meaning for herself.

On the ground floor, next to the stalls of goats, sheep, and chickens, she sat with the children to hear Lemuel, the boy from Capernaum, tell his tale.

"We're here for Passover," Lemuel began. "Every year my father says, 'This year, Jerusalem for Passover.' But we stay home. Then he heard Yeshua would be in Jerusalem this Passover. Lo and behold, here we are. We're staying with my mother's cousin."

Samuel and Simon urged him to get

on with the story.

"Well, it happened just a few weeks ago in Capernaum. This huge crowd was gathered around a little hill just outside of town, near the harbor. I was on my way home. I had my cast-net and a couple of fish I caught for supper. Nothing much, just a barbel and a musht. Not big, not little. About this size. My mother told me to stop by the baker's oven to pick up the five barley loaves she left. So I had these two fish on a string and a basket of bread when the one they call Andrew came up to me and said . . ."

"Who's Andrew?" asked Sarah.

"He must be one of Yeshua's followers," Zebedee offered.

"That's right," said the new boy. "He's not too tall and his hair is . . ."

"Just get on with the story, please," Rachel pleaded.

"Okay. Well, anyway, Andrew said to me, 'Boy, you see that man talking to all those people? Well, he wants me to ask you for a

donation. He needs this food from you, okay?'
Now I couldn't really see the man over all
those heads, but I knew he must be important,
you know? So I followed Andrew in and out of
the people. Finally we came close to where this
man was standing. He was preaching in a loud,
booming voice. I said, 'Okay, he can have my
loaves and fish,' even though I figured I was
going to be in big trouble when I got home.

"There was a fire going, and Andrew put
the fish on to roast. Next thing I knew, he was
telling me to help him pass out the food. He
took the fish; I took the bread."

"To feed a big crowd of people?" Rachel
was incredulous.

"Could have been five million, I don't
know. They said afterward it was five thousand,
I don't know. But I tell you what, they had a
whole lot more people than I had food."

"Let the boy continue, Rachel," scolded
Uncle Ezra. "As I believe you requested."

"Oh, yeah. Before we got started, this
preacher, Yeshua, the Master, he sat everybody

down in the grass and said a prayer over my
baskets. Then me and Andrew started passing
around the food. Everybody broke off a chunk
of fish and a chunk of bread and we gave the
baskets to the next one. And (Lemuel's voice
grew more excited), and listen to this: No
matter how many people we served, we never
ran out! We must have passed around bread
and fish for an hour. And when Andrew
handed me back the baskets, guess what? There
were *three* fish and *seven* loaves of bread! I got
back more than I gave. We sure ate good at my
house that night."

"A miracle!" Elizabeth exclaimed, her
voice full of wonder.

"So, uh, so it would seem," said Uncle
Ezra into his beard. "So it would seem."

"I have to go now," said Lemuel, getting
to his feet. "My father promised to take me to
the temple. He says Yeshua's going to be there,
and that's why we're here. He wants to see this
miracle man for himself. We're going to
sacrifice some pigeons, maybe."

MIRACLE IN JERUSALEM

"You think he'll take us too?" Zebedee asked, pulling Samuel and Simon up from the ground.

"We can ask him," agreed Lemuel, turning to leave.

As the boys ran toward the street, Uncle Ezra called out, "Tell your father to buy his pigeons from old Malachi, three doors down. Tell him those vendors in the temple charge outrageous prices. They gouge the tourists. Old Malachi, eh?"

As Uncle Ezra dusted himself off, Sarah and Rachel were helping Elizabeth to her feet. *The child looks worse today*, Ezra thought. Her strength was waning.

"Oh, look," said Elizabeth. "Lemuel left his hat." She picked up a dusty striped cap from the floor just in time, for the nanny goat was eyeing it hungrily. "I think I'll run and catch him."

"You'll do no such thing," her mother snapped. "Back upstairs with you, the way you've been coughing . . ."

"I'll take it to him," Sarah offered.

Elizabeth clutched the cap close to her breast. "Oh, no," she said. "If I can't take it myself, I'll keep it right here. That way he'll have to come back and get it."

"You like him!" Sarah teased. "Lizzy's got a boyfriend. Lizzy's got a boyfriend."

Elizabeth stuck out her tongue and said, "Don't be stupid, Sarah. I just think it's interesting, you know, the way he helped Yeshua and all. You know."

"Lizzy and Lemuel. Hah!"

"Shut up, Sarah."

"That's enough out of both of you," Rachel scolded. "Sarah, you help me get Elizabeth tucked in. She needs to catch up on her rest after whatever it was you two got into yesterday."

As they boosted Elizabeth up the short ladder to the main room of the house, Sarah asked Rachel, "Do you think Yeshua really can make miracles happen?"

Hearing no answer, she prattled on.

"What do you think, Lizzy? I mean, he touched you yesterday, didn't he? He fed all those hungry people and makes deaf people hear and lame people walk. So? So maybe he can make you well, huh? What do you think, Lizzy?"

Elizabeth stopped and looked down at her friend. "Well, maybe so. Maybe he can. And you know what else he could do, Sarah?"

"What?"

"He could make you keep quiet for a minute. Now that really would be a miracle!"

Rachel and Uncle Ezra burst into laughter and immediately Sarah was laughing right along with them. As she watched her friend Elizabeth struggle to pull herself up to the landing, Sarah thought, *Nobody makes people smile the way Lizzy does. Nobody.* Then she realized, with a start, *Even that Roman soldier smiled.*

At that moment, Rachel was thinking much the same thing. Between Jew and Roman she had seen only hatred, fear, and mistrust. Even when, as a child, she offered sanctuary to

the soldier, they both had been fearful and
wary of one another.

Maybe there is a power in her weakness,
Rachel wondered. *Maybe innocence and love are
kinds of miracles that can turn fear into trust.*

PASS IT ON DOWN

Five loaves of bread, two little fishes.
Take what you need, pass it on down.
Five loaves of bread, two little fishes.
Just enough to go around.

Shake someone's hand, nice to have met
      you.
Take what you need, pass it on down.
Shake someone's hand, sure won't forget you.
Hands enough to go around.

Pat on the back, cheer on a neighbor.
Take what you need, pass it on down.
Help out a friend, share in his labor.
Work enough to go around.

Give me a hug, good to be near you.
Take what you need, pass it on down.
Long as we're close, ain't gonna fear you.
Hugs enough to go around.

Songs in the air, hear all the voices.
Take what you need, pass it on down.
Songs everywhere, so many choices.
Songs enough to go around.

Feels good to share, gives me a tingle.
Take what you need, pass it on down.
Takes two to share, beats being single.
Folks enough to go around.

Love comes from God, don't you refuse it.
Take what you need, pass it on down.
Take what you need, learn how to use it.
Love enough to go around.

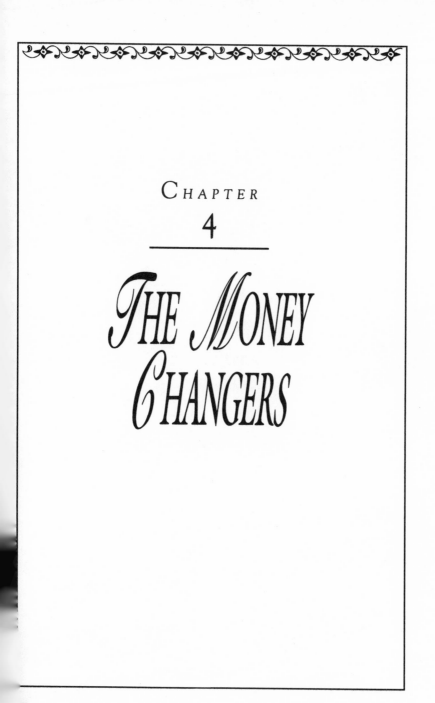

CHAPTER
4

THE MONEY CHANGERS

*W*hat with calling on relatives and shopping at the big market, Lemuel's family did not get to the temple until almost noon. By that time, *a few friends* had turned into all six of the orphan children. But the streets were so filled with pilgrims in the city for Passover week, it was hard to tell who went with whom, and the tagalongs were scarcely noticed by Lemuel's father.

As she neared the magnificent temple complex, Sarah looked up. She had to shade her eyes from the glare of the sun as it reflected off the white marble and beaten gold of the outer walls. Hanging on to Margaret's sleeve, she was swept along in the current of the crowd, through the Royal Porticoes and up the broad stone steps to the raised courtyard. They were standing in the Court of the Gentiles.

Sarah had been inside the temple walls only twice before. It was a magical place. The wide courtyard was filled with so many people in strange costumes speaking strange languages, it was like visiting a foreign land.

Even though the Festival of Unleavened Bread was just three days away, and the routine of city life was breaking down into holiday confusion, construction work on the temple itself went on. Stonemasons, bricklayers, and carpenters were hard at their jobs. The work of building the new temple had been going on for more than forty years now, Uncle Ezra said, and no one had a guess when it would be completed. It seemed complete enough to Sarah just the way it was.

To the right, lining the long Eastern Wall, was an almost endless arcade of shops and stalls and booths. Normally, there was room to stroll about, to play hide-and-seek among the columns, to pet the lambs, and to listen to the lofty conversations of old men. But today every shop was crammed with visitors for Passover. There was barely room to walk.

Their first stop was a money-changing booth, where Lemuel's father stood in line to exchange the Roman coins he used in Galilee for the coins of Jerusalem, called *shekels*. If you wanted to buy something to offer to the Lord, or even just wanted to drop something into the temple treasury box, the Law said you had to use shekels. In Jerusalem, Sarah was convinced, there was a law for every occasion. Sarah noticed that at the money table every man or woman would argue about the rate of exchange. They all thought they should receive more shekels than the dealers gave them. No matter how many times a foreigner might hear others lose this argument, when it came his turn at the table he had to lose it for himself.

Grownups can be ridiculous, Sarah reminded herself.

There were voices singing in the distance. Sarah had to know who was making all the noise. Pulling Margaret and Rebecca with her, she climbed the wooden gate of an oxen stall. From here they could see above the heads of the throng and take in the entire scene.

They could see the Women's Court and the Altar of Burnt Offering. Just below the High Porch and the Court of the Priests, on wide curving stairs, a group of white-robed men stood and sang together. They were Levites, singing the *Shir Hamaaloth* from the Psalms of David:

I rejoiced when they said to me,
"Let us go to the house of the Lord."
Now we stand within your gates,
O Jerusalem:
Jerusalem that is built to be a city
Where people come together in unity.

"They sure are coming together today," chirped Rebecca.

Zebedee was shouting to them. "Come on, girls. We're heading over to the bird shops."

"Oh, well," said Sarah. "I guess Lemuel forgot to tell his papa about the lower prices at old Malachi's."

They were starting to climb down when Margaret said, "Hey, what's that?"

There was a great hubbub over near the Royal Porticoes. Men and women were pushing and shoving, surging forward. Then, even as it was converging, the crowd began to split, making way for a column of men who were shouting at the tops of their lungs: "Blessings on him who comes as king in the name of the Lord! Peace in heaven! Glory in the highest heaven! Blessings on our master."

The three girls stood on the gatepost, craning their necks. Rebecca was first to spot the center of all this commotion. "It's him!" she cried. "It's Yeshua!"

Now many people near to the girls' perch

began talking and pointing excitedly. Just a few yards away, the great stone doors of the Sanhedrin chamber pushed open and the leading elders of the city emerged, squinting in the bright sunlight, to find out the cause of the disturbance.

Pharisees ran in chattering bunches, their long, embroidered robes hiked up to protect the elaborate hems. As they ran, their great bushy curls flew out like kite tails from each ear.

Wealthy Sadducees, chests hung with gold, fingers heavy with precious stones, shielded their eyes from the sudden sunlight. They took hurried little skip-steps, hoping no one would notice that such important men were actually running. Priests rushed out in nervous pairs, and clerks followed, still clutching their writing tablets.

Sarah thought, *Everybody wants to find out what this man from Nazareth has to say.*

But the crowd was pressed deep around Yeshua and his band, too deep for the Sanhedrin officials to push through. While the

city's big shots craned their necks and stood on
tiptoes, Margaret, Rebecca, and Sarah watched
from a superior vantage point. They had a clear
view of Yeshua as he strode to the same
money-changing booth where Lemuel's father
had waited in line.

"Look," cried Sarah, "he's arguing just like
everyone else."

But Yeshua was not arguing over the price
of shekels. Although they could not hear his
words clearly, there was no mistaking the anger
in the teacher's hoarse voice. Sarah made out
phrases like "my father's house" and "hangout
for thieves and cutthroats."

Suddenly tables were flying and money was
jangling in every direction. Some people fell to
the ground and fought each other over the
spinning gold and silver coins. Sarah was ready
to jump down and join the scuffle, but
Margaret held her back. "Too dangerous," she
shouted. "Stay up here."

"Besides," said Rebecca, "we can't miss
the rest of the show."

Indeed, most people in the crowd must have felt the same way for they were cheering on the tall, thin Yeshua like an athlete in the arena.

Now Yeshua was charging from one shop to another, kicking over tables, breaking cages, and opening stalls. Pigeons and doves went flapping in every direction. Goats and geese and lambs butted and squawked and squealed between legs and behind columns.

Sarah, Margaret, and Rebecca were squealing, too, in delight. It was grand!

But as Yeshua came closer, Sarah grew frightened. The young oxen in the stall behind her were stamping and blowing nervously. What if she should lose her balance and fall back into the stall?

Then she heard: "Margaret, Sarah, Reba! Come on, let's get out of here. Things are getting too rough."

It was Zebedee. He reached up to lift them to the ground, one by one. Joining hands with Simon, Samuel, and Lemuel to form a chain,

the girls snaked through the tumult toward the
gate, Zebedee leading the way. As they bumped
and pushed and squeezed through the shouting
crowd, Sarah could still hear the voices of the
Levites rising in the background:

For thy servant David's sake
Reject not thy anointed king.
The Lord swore to David
An oath he will not break:
"A prince of your own line
Will I set upon your throne."

What an adventure! Sarah thought. She
could barely wait to tell Lizzy about it.

LITTLE CHILDREN COME TO ME

Did you hear him say
Children know the way?
Let the little children come to me.
Let the girls and boys
Make their joyful noise.
Let the little children come to me.

Life is God's to give,
So let the children live.
Let the little children come to me.
Take his gift and smile
Like a grateful child.
Let the little children come to me.

I'm gonna sing and shout and clap,
Climb up in his lap, 'cause he said,
Let the little children come to me.

Watch the children play,
Soon you'll learn the way.
Let the little children come to me.
Be a child again,
You'll see heaven then.
Let the little children come to me.

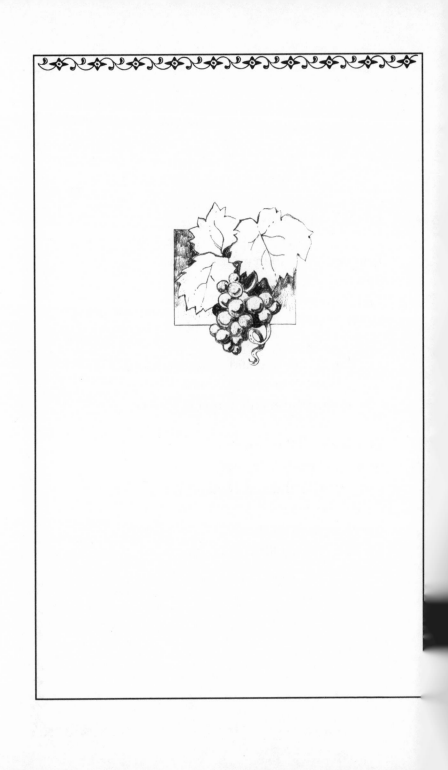

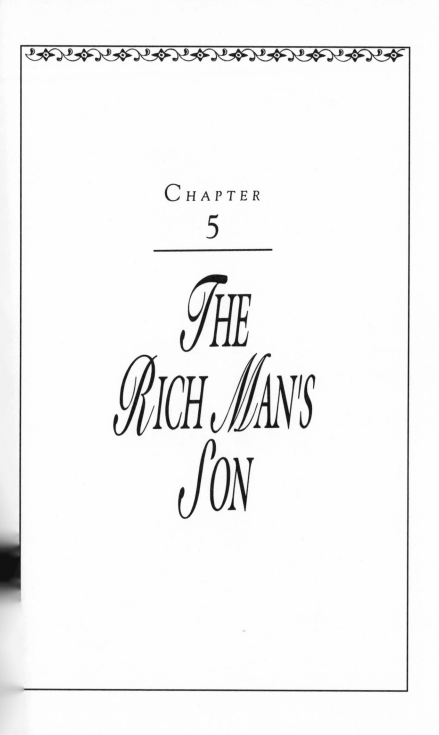

CHAPTER
5

THE
RICH MAN'S
SON

*B*ut who is this man?" asked Rachel, after listening carefully to the wild tale of the temple outburst. "What sort of person is this Yeshua?"

Naturally the children all had their opinions, which they voiced first all together, then by twos and threes, and eventually one by one.

"Prophet."

"He's like an army general."

"No, a big rabbi. Well, he *is*!"

"They're gonna make him the king."

"A new high priest."

Only Samuel and Simon, as usual, were in perfect agreement. "Incredible!" they said in unison.

Elizabeth, who was feeling much better after resting most of yesterday, applauded the brothers' vote.

Rachel noticed that her uncle was unusually thoughtful. So she asked, "What about you, Uncle Ezra?"

The old man tugged at his beard and stuck out his lower lip. "Hmm," he said, "weeell." He lowered his paunchy frame to the floor and stretched out, resting his head on an elbow-propped fist. "Don't, uh, mmm . . . don't see how I can disagree with any of those learned opinions."

"But what about your own opinion?" Elizabeth insisted.

"Have you heard Yeshua preach yet?" Rachel asked.

"Oh yes, yes indeed. That I have. Only

this morning."

Elizabeth rolled over to lean against Ezra's big pillowy stomach and batted her lashes at him. She loved to hear her uncle's stories, and she knew he loved to be begged for them. Sarah imitated Uncle Ezra on the floor, elbows propping up her chin.

After much *ahem*-ing and grunting and *weeell*-ing, Uncle Ezra agreed to relate the tale told by the visitor Yeshua to a group of old men, including a number of priests and Pharisees. Uncle Ezra said the men had given Yeshua their undivided attention and that he expected that same attention now.

"We'll be quiet," Elizabeth promised.

"Very well, then," said Uncle Ezra. Pulling his prayer shawl around his shoulders and hunching forward, he took a deep and important breath and began the story.

"There once was a rich man who lived in the big city. He had some money to invest, and he decided to buy some country property, maybe a farm with a vineyard that could make more money for him. After all, he was a businessman, and he felt, um, well, that his investments should turn an honest profit.

"So he found a beautiful estate, with, oh, rolling hills covered with excellent grape vines. And wouldn't you know, it was for sale—at a price the gentleman considered fair. He bought it and hired a manager and workers to keep it going and produce good wine. The workers could live on the estate, you see, and they would receive a nice percentage of the profits when the wine was sold.

"Well, ah, a year went by, then two, and at last the wine was ready to be put up in jars and sold, you see. A fine, full-bodied wine it was, too, and it brought top shekel at the market.

"Back home in the city, the, ah, businessman waited for his manager to turn in the profits. He waited and waited. Finally he sent his secretary to see what the delay was about. Next day, well, the secretary came back with his head bandaged and his arm in a sling.

THE RICH MAN'S SON

'They beat me up and threw me out,' he told the rich man. 'They claim they did all the work and now they will keep all the profits.'

"Well! Needless to say, our businessman was, so to speak, not pleased. Still, he felt the vineyard workers were capable people who could be persuaded to do a good job. So he called in his son and said, 'Son, get down there and tell those people I'm giving them one more chance. Explain to them the error of their ways. You tell them they can stay on, but only if they send us our share of the profits. Right now. If they don't, I'm going to be very angry. Tell them I mean business.'

"And the son did as he was told.

"But when the estate manager called his people in to give them the news, they just laughed. 'Let's show the old man *we* mean business!' one of them shouted. So they took up their hoes and shovels and rakes and dragged the owner's son outside the vineyard, and they beat him. They beat him until he was dead."

Elizabeth gasped and one of the boys started to speak, but a raised finger from Uncle Ezra told them the story was not over, not yet.

The old man continued in a low and menacing voice.

"And what do you suppose the vineyard owner did then, eh? Well, for a few days he mourned his son, of course. Then he called a meeting of all the people who worked for him in the city. He said, 'I made a very bad investment.' He sent his people in the night to kill the manager and the workers, every last one. And then he went and found somebody else to take care of that estate."

Uncle Ezra rose from the mat and drank from the ladle in the water jar. Rachel sat silent, staring at Elizabeth, whose eyes were wide with wonder.

"What does it mean?" she asked. Elizabeth was accustomed to eavesdropping on street-corner rabbis as they "explained" the stories from the Torah. In Jerusalem, storytelling was the most important form of communication.

News, history, school lessons, even the Law
passed from one to another through stories like
this. Consequently, Elizabeth expected every
good story to have a "meaning."

"What does it mean, eh? That, my child,
is exactly what the priests asked themselves this
morning. What does it mean?" Uncle Ezra took
another gulp of water and wiped his gray beard.
"Mmm. Yes. What does it mean?"

"What if the vineyard is Israel?" asked
Rebecca.

"What if the rich man is Yahweh?" asked
Margaret.

"Yes, yes," said Uncle Ezra thoughtfully.
"And who is the son who is put to death,
mmm? And who are the workers who kill
him?"

Zebedee sat up, cross-legged on the floor,
Simon and Samuel on either side of him.
"Those are good questions, Uncle. But you still
have not shared your opinion. Who do *you*
think this man Yeshua is?"

"What I think . . ." Uncle Ezra paused.

"I think . . . hmmm. I am afraid to think what I think. This man may be, may be *all* the things you've said and, uh, more. But one occupation I will vouch for—he is a fine teacher. The finest teacher I have ever encountered."

"A *teacher*," groaned Samuel and Simon.

"Just a teacher?" pleaded Rebecca.

"Oh, now, wait a minute." Uncle Ezra frowned and glared around the room. "Did I say *just* a teacher? I did not. There is no *just* about it at all. A call to teaching is, well, a mighty great call.

"Just think of all the things a teacher can teach, eh? Why, aren't those as many as the things to be learned? All the wonders of the earth and sea and sky. Well, don't you know, I've thought about becoming a teacher myself someday. When I get old, I mean."

"But you're already . . ." Simon and Samuel burst out. It was all Zeb could do to slap a palm across each of their mouths. He did not wait to see whether they considered Uncle

Ezra a teacher or simply an old man.

Instead, Zeb asked a question of his own. "What about all those miracles, Uncle Ezra? All that healing and curing? Teachers don't go around doing stuff like that."

"He's a doctor," burst out Sarah. "A really great doctor. I bet he could cure Lizzy right now!"

"Oh, now, wait," said Uncle Ezra, fumbling for words. "Maybe we shouldn't . . ."

But Sarah was pulling Elizabeth to her feet, ready to dance for joy. "Mama?" questioned Elizabeth. "Do you think . . ."

"I don't know," said Rachel. "A man like that. So many important things to do. He wouldn't like being bothered with the problems of an ordinary little girl."

"Lizzy's not ordinary," Sarah protested.

"Neither is Yeshua," Lemuel said softly. "I've listened to all your opinions, and you're wrong. Yeshua may be all the things you say, but he's much more than that. My father believes he's the Messiah."

A hush fell upon the room. The children looked to Rachel and Uncle Ezra. Israel had been awaiting a deliverer for a long, long time. Could this really be the one? At last, it was Rachel who spoke. "Well, what if he *is* the Messiah? And with the whole nation to save, you think he has time for my poor little girl?"

"I know he does," answered Lemuel. " 'Cause he said once nobody should keep the boys and girls from bothering him. He said, 'Let the little children come to me.' "

Sarah whispered conspiratorially: "Psst, Lizzy! I think Lemuel likes you too."

Rachel smiled and got to her feet. "If Yeshua practices what he preaches, perhaps we should just go see what he has to say about this young lady of ours."

"All *right*!" said Samuel and Simon together. And Sarah whooped.

"But let's just wait a few days," Rachel added calmly. "Just until the Passover celebration is over and things quiet down a bit."

So much going on these days, Rachel

thought as the children said their good-byes. *So much excitement, with Passover and the man from Galilee.*

"Oh no," said Elizabeth. "I forgot to give back Lemuel's hat!"

"Don't worry," Rachel answered with a smile, "I have a feeling we'll see him again."

TEACHERS

A teacher knows things
that need to be learned.
A teacher knows things
that need to be burned in your brain.

A teacher knows what
makes everything run,
Knows what it takes
to turn on the sunshine or rain.

A teacher who dares
can overcome fear.
A teacher who cares
makes mysteries clear for us children.

Teachers unlock the doors
that open our hearts,
They kindle the flames,
and sometimes they start up a fire.

A teacher can teach
us, whether or not
We quite understand
that we're being taught to go higher.

A teacher who's kind
will give us a shove.
So go out and find
a teacher who'll love us as children.

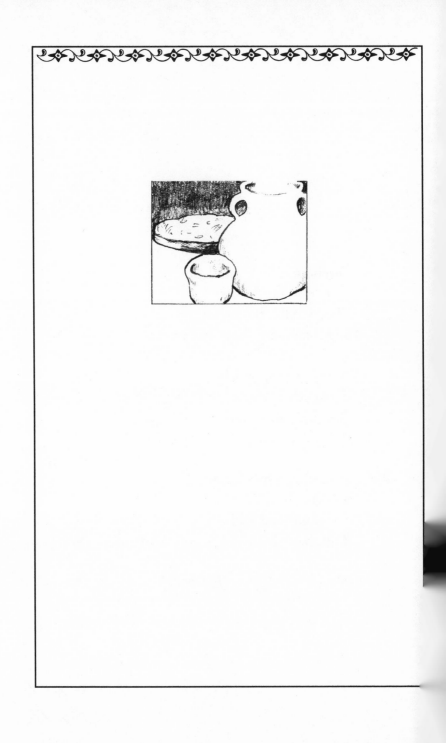

CHAPTER

6

JEDER
NEWS

*A*t first Rachel smiled at the way Elizabeth threw herself into the work. She loved preparing the special Passover meal, called the Seder. Even the housecleaning seemed like fun when a girl could keep her mind on the great celebration to come, with all the delicious food and the singing of songs and the telling of stories that this joyous night would bring.

But before long Elizabeth seemed to grow so tired and weak from all the activity that

Rachel insisted she lie still and leave the chores to the orphan girls.

Preparation of the holiday meal was supposed to be a joyous time, especially for the women of the Hebrew household. But as the day wore on it was all Rachel could do to keep from crying at the sight of her poor little girl. Every now and then Elizabeth would have a coughing spell that racked her frail body, and Rachel wondered whether she'd even be able to sit through the long meal.

Margaret, Rebecca, and Sarah were more quiet than usual as they bustled about, preparing the maror and the special herbs. But Elizabeth was quick to break what was threatening to become a somber mood.

"Now I know how it feels to be a boy," she said. "I just lie here in comfort while the women get the work done. Of course the silly boys will probably think this dinner cooked itself. *I* will know better."

Rachel had invited all the orphan children to join them, as she frequently did on special occasions. The Feast of the Unleavened Bread was one of the most festive times in the year, and she never let the children miss out on it. Uncle Ezra would be there, of course—he had bought the special lamb and taken it to the temple for preparation by the priests. There were so many rituals and traditions attached to Passover.

As Rachel was chopping onions and herbs, there was a knock at the door. It was Lemuel, the boy from Capernaum, and he was carrying a wineskin. "A gift from my family," he said, "for your Seder."

"That is so very thoughtful and kind," said Rachel with a smile. She suspected this gift had been Lemuel's own idea. Perhaps Sarah was right about this young man and his feelings toward Elizabeth.

"My mother says it's you who is kind and thoughtful," replied Lemuel. "Taking care of all the orphans the way you do. And my father says widows don't have a lot of money."

Rachel did not correct Lemuel. If they

knew she was a divorced woman, his family might take back the wine. Let them think she was a widow.

"As for the children," she replied, "I do it for Lizzy here. They're her friends, and they help keep her from getting underfoot. Isn't that right, Elizabeth?" The girl started to answer but fell into a coughing spasm and could only nod. Rachel asked if Lemuel would stay and take supper with them.

"No, thank you," the Galilean boy replied. "I wish I could, but we're having supper with my mother's cousins. And guess what, Lizzy! Right down the street from their house is the place where Yeshua and his friends are supposed to be staying tonight."

"Really?" asked Elizabeth in a raspy voice. "If you see him, will you ask him to come over here and fix me up?"

"Good idea!" said Margaret. "Ask him, Lemuel."

"I might just do that." He turned to go, then spoke again, in Elizabeth's direction. "Um,

I think we have to leave tomorrow, to go home. But I hope we can still be, you know, friends."

"You bet!" said Sarah. She winked at Lizzy. "*Good* friends."

"And next year you'll share a Passover meal with us," Rachel offered. "All right?"

"And I'll be running around so much you won't recognize me," said Lizzy, sitting taller on her straw mat. "It's been nice meeting you, Lemuel."

"Nice meeting you, too, Lizzy. Oh, I mean you, too. *Everybody*."

Sarah grinned. In a sing-songy voice she asked, "Aren't you forgetting something, Lizzy?"

"What? Oh! Your cap. You left it here, Lemuel."

Rachel took the cap from a shelf and handed it to the round-faced boy. His cheeks reddened as he accepted it. "I, uh, wouldn't mind if you kept it," he said. "But thanks for giving it back. See you."

When Lemuel had gone, Rachel sent the

giggling orphan girls up to the rooftop to finish
setting the table. The rooftop was cool and
airy, the perfect place for special occasions like
Passover. She walked over to Elizabeth and sat
down at the edge of her straw mat. "You like
him, don't you?" she asked.

"Mmm-hmm," said Elizabeth. "He's funny,
but he's kind of sweet. I feel sad that he's
going."

"You shouldn't be sad. After all . . ."

"But, in a way," Lizzy interrupted, "I'm
almost glad to be sad. Know what I mean? It's
kind of a burning feeling. It hurts, but it makes
you warm."

Rachel went back to work, setting out
candles for the meal. "It's because he touched
you in a special way," she said.

"It's like lighting a candle, Mama. When
you touch it with a glowing straw and then
you take the straw away, the candle still
burns where the straw touched it. Losing
Lemuel is better than never having found
him. You know?"

The other girls, coming back into the room, looked at each other in a serious way. Margaret nodded.

"I think I understand," said Rachel. "And now I hear some of our men arriving. Elizabeth, if you get to feeling worse, just take yourself off to sleep."

"Don't worry," said Elizabeth, looking up with her dark, hollow eyes. "I'll be fine. Where's the special cup for Elijah? Don't let Sarah carry it. She'll probably drop it or something."

*U*ncle Ezra arrived first, making a great show of going to the oven, taking slow, solemn strides like a priest to the altar. He opened the oven door to inspect the portion of lamb left over after the ritual sacrifice and donation to the temple priests. Uncle Ezra inhaled deeply, three times, then let out a resounding proclamation. "The finest roast of lamb in all Jerusalem!"

Zebedee, Simon, and Samuel came in just moments later. All the children crowded close behind him as Uncle Ezra climbed to the roof and carefully counted the places. "Only nine at dinner? There must be at least ten—ten *men*," he protested. "Tradition demands it!"

Elizabeth pointed out that there was only one actual man in the company, unless they counted Zebedee, who was fourteen years old. Uncle Ezra said that under certain circumstances, women and girls could be counted. "But what about number ten?"

"I know," said Sarah. "Let's set a place for Elijah, and he can be number ten!"

Everyone thought that was a grand idea, particularly since it was customary to put out a wine glass for the prophet in case he happened to drop in. Tradition said that one Passover night Elijah would come back to herald the arrival of the Messiah, the deliverer of Israel. Observing tradition was one of the best things about Passover.

So, as the sun went down on the

fourteenth day of the month of Nisan, just as
tradition demanded, Rachel lit the candles.
Margaret, Rebecca, and Sarah began to serve
the traditional foods at the rooftop table, the
traditional place for traditional celebrations.

They reclined on mats around the long,
low, narrow table, Uncle Ezra at one end and
Zebedee at the other. Since Zebedee
represented the eldest son of the family, it was
his duty to begin by asking the traditional
questions.

"This night, this night, how does it differ
from all other nights in the year?"

They all knew the answer, but it was
tradition to keep silent. Uncle Ezra would
provide the answers at the proper time. Then
Zebedee raised a clay bowl containing a
mixture of lettuce and herbs. "These herbs,
these herbs," he intoned in a sing-songy voice,
"so tart and so bitter, why must we eat them
this night of the year?" Again there was no
answer.

Zebedee took up a carefully folded napkin

and raised it above his head. Inside the napkin
was a flat cake of matzo, bread baked without
any yeast to make it rise. He asked the evening
sky, "This bread, this bread that is flat and
unleavened, why do we break it this night of
the year?"

Now Uncle Ezra stood and began the
telling of the Passover story. It was a tale they
all knew, but one they must hear every year of
their lives. The boys, Zebedee, Simon, and
Samuel, must learn every word by heart. When
they had families of their own, they must be
able to repeat the words precisely for their sons
to learn. The story began with the ancient
Hebrew words of praise to the Lord.

Ba-ruch a-taw, a-do-noi, e-lo-hay-nu!
Praised be God for this Promised Land.
And for this night, to rejoice, to remember
All we owe to His mighty hand.

Uncle Ezra was chanting the story of
Yahweh's deliverance of the Hebrews from

slavery in Egypt. This was the great turning
point in Jewish history.

He felt our grief, beheld our oppression.
He heard our cries and our weary groans.
He felt the lash on the backs of His children,
Saw our blood and our broken bones.
At last spoke our Lord to the arrogant Pharaoh:
Be ye cursed, be thy name reviled!
For on this night, in each house of thy kingdom,
I shall slay every firstborn child.

Now Uncle Ezra rose and his voice boomed
across the rooftop.

And in the night He sent His awful sword,
the righteous anger of the Lord.
The streets were filled with wailing,
and the air was filled with dread.
But in the night His hand passed over us,
His mighty hand passed over us.
And morning saw that Egypt's
firstborn children all lay dead.

The old man paused, lowered himself to the floor again, and took a sip of sweet red wine. After he drank, he passed the cup to the others and they each took a sip; such was the custom. Uncle Ezra returned to his narrative.

Then we set out from the land of the Pharaoh;
Made we haste for the desert sand.
There was no time for our bread to be leavened,
Such was our haste for the Promised Land.
Ba-ruch a-taw, a-do-noi, e-lo-hay-nu!
We give thanks, mighty Lord, to Thee!

He signaled for the others to join him, and they chanted together.

Ba-ruch a-taw, a-do-noi, e-lo-hay-nu!
For it was you, mighty Lord, who set us free.

Once again Uncle Ezra passed around a cup of wine. When everyone had drunk, he raised his hands to recite an old prayer.

May He who is most merciful be adored through all generations. May He who is most merciful send abundant blessings upon this house. May He who is most merciful send us Elijah, the prophet of blessed memory.

And so the praying and the ceremony continued. Uncle Ezra passed the wine cups and the bowls of special food: the bitter herbs, reminders of the bitter years of bondage in Egypt; the crisp, crackly matzo to remind them of the haste in which their ancestors were forced to flee Egypt, with not even time enough to let the bread rise in the ovens; the maror, a mixture of apples and raisins and spices, to make them think of the bricks and mortar their ancestors were forced to make for their captors.

Finally came the lamb, like the lamb their ancestors had slain, to mark the doorpost with its blood, so that the angel of death would pass over them. The roasted lamb was fragrant with mint and rosemary, and no one thought to dispute Uncle Ezra's claim that it was, indeed, the finest in Jerusalem that night.

*A*fter dinner there were more songs to be sung, prayers to be recited, and stories to be told. Elizabeth missed most of these, falling asleep shortly after a few bites of the main course. One by one, the other children followed her example, simply rolling over on their mats and laying their heads on their arms.

The candles burned down and flickered out. Uncle Ezra was snoring, his big head rising and falling to the rhythm of his full belly. Only Rachel remained awake, cradling Lizzy's head in her lap. She looked up and saw the heaven filled with stars, dazzling, twinkling, and throbbing with secret energy.

Rachel recalled how her grandmother once believed the stars held magic powers. Rachel doubted that. Yet things beyond explanation do occur. Why? How? Perhaps the stars in fact control human destiny. Perhaps, if she wished

upon the stars, her beautiful daughter would get
well, would grow strong and healthy.

She made that wish, but it seemed to her
a hopeless wish. If miracles happened, then it
would be the Lord who made them happen.
She believed in Yahweh, not in the stars.

Rachel had been praying to the Lord for
years, mostly out of her love for Elizabeth. *If I
pray,* she thought, *then perhaps I do have hope. I
must have hope. Perhaps it is* faith *I lack.*

At last, her head filled with questions and
her heart filled with uncertain fear, Rachel fell
asleep under the stars. She dreamed of running
like the swift night wind, faster than a camel
across the desert. And Lizzy, glowing with a
new life, was running right beside her. On and
on they ran, faster and faster, until the soles of
their bare feet no longer touched the sliding
grains of sand. Now they were flying . . .

"Rachel, wake up! Wake up, please!"

Someone was shaking her. She awoke with
a start to find Lemuel, without a stitch of
clothes on. He was shivering, naked as a shorn

sheep, and in his eyes there was a look of terror.

"He's been arrested!"

"Who's been arrested?" Rachel demanded, getting to her feet. "What are you doing with no clothes on?" She wrapped Lemuel in a shawl and got him some water. His frantic whispers had awakened the others. They were rolling over, rubbing their eyes, and wondering if it could be morning already.

Lemuel caught his breath and told his story.

"I slipped away. Everyone at my uncle's house was asleep. I was wearing my nightshirt. I wanted to see Yeshua, to ask him about Lizzy. I had to try before we went home.

"But when I got to the house where they were staying, they were all gone. A lady told me they went to the Mount of Olives. So I ran after them.

"They were all in a little garden up there, all but Yeshua, and the others were sound asleep. So I hid in some bushes. All at once I

heard a noise, like a crowd coming. And there
was Yeshua, standing in the garden, shaking
the one they call Peter.

"Before I knew what was happening, there
was this angry mob in the garden, trampling
flowers and swinging swords and clubs. They
said Yeshua was under arrest. His men started
fighting with them. A lot of blood. Yeshua just
went quietly, you know? But everybody else ran
away.

"Then somebody yelled, 'There's another
one, in the bushes!' and he meant me! So I
ran, and he made a leap for me. But all he got
was my nightshirt."

From a corner of the room, Sarah giggled,
but Rachel stopped her with a look. "It's not
funny!" Lemuel shouted, close to tears.
"They've got him. I think they're going to kill
him. *They're going to kill Yeshua!*"

RACHEL'S WISH

I wish I knew why the Lord above
made a child so full of life and love.
    Was it just to let her waste away?
    Was it just to hear a mother pray?

Wish I didn't have to tell her "no."
Wish her life was hanging by a stronger thread.
Wish I could do more. Wish we weren't poor.
Wish she had a pillow and a feather bed.

Wish I didn't have to tell her "no."
Wish that I could buy her all the pretty toys.
Wish I could be sure God would send a cure.
Wish that she could play like all the girls and
    boys.

Wish I didn't have to tell her "no."
Wish that I could laugh to see her running by.
But I feel her heart,
Hear her breath run short.
Wish I didn't know that she was born to die.

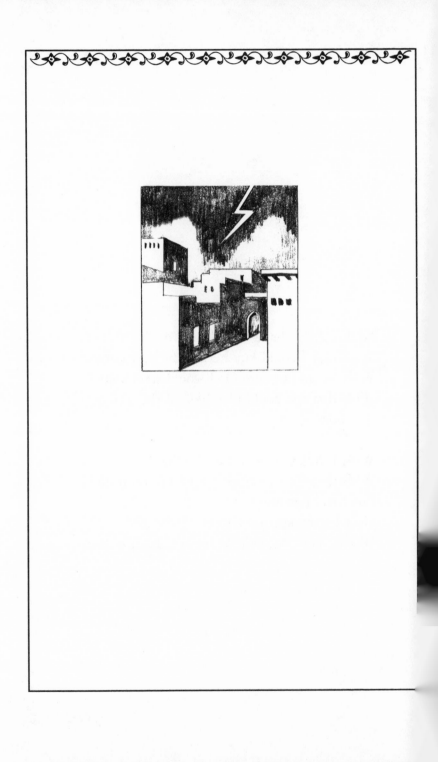

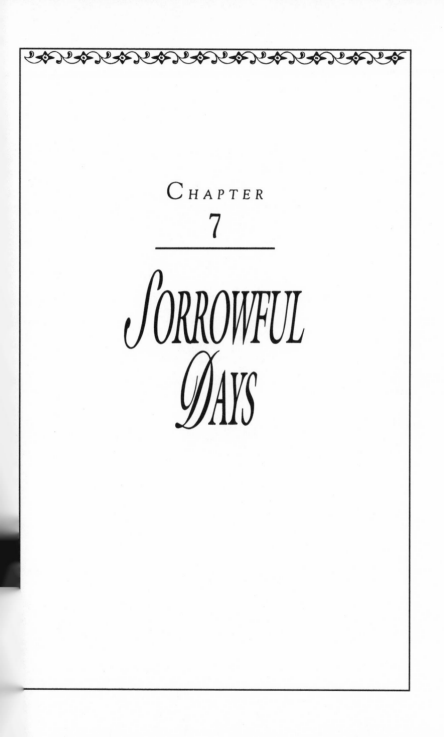

CHAPTER

7

SORROWFUL DAYS

*T*he next day was Friday, and everyone arose late. After Lemuel left, they'd all had trouble getting back to sleep. As a result they got up cranky. The sun was hidden behind gray and gloomy clouds, which only made matters worse.

Elizabeth's condition was worse also. Her new friend Lemuel, who seemed to have a mystical connection to the man called Yeshua, was gone on the long journey back to Capernaum. Rachel wondered if he would

indeed return next Passover and whether
Elizabeth would still be here to see him. *How
much longer can she go on like this?* she
wondered.

One by one, the orphans trickled from the
house, scratching their heads and yawning,
kicking up little puffs of dust in the street.

Sarah went to Amram the Potter's to
collect lumps of clay from the ground around
his wheel. She had a notion to take them back
to Elizabeth so they could make doll-sized
plates and bowls together. But as she walked
along, she found her fingers just picking at the
clay and tossing it away, bit by bit. There was
just no play in her.

Simon was of a mind to steal old Mina's
donkey and go for a ride, but Samuel said he'd
rather walk if they had any place to walk to,
which they didn't. It was the first time the
brothers could remember not agreeing, but they
weren't in a mood to make much of that,
either.

So they agreed to do nothing.

That afternoon the sky turned even darker, and there were ferocious rumblings, like thunderclouds rolling in from far away. But there was no lightning, and there was no rain.

Margaret and Rebecca tagged along behind Zebedee, who was just following a crowd of people. They went to the governor's palace where a big meeting was going on. The girls returned to Rachel's house at suppertime with little appetite and less to say.

A sudden thunderclap went off like a roar in Rachel's ear and made her drop a bowl. It was a bowl her grandmother had turned years ago and passed down as an heirloom. It lay shattered in a thousand pieces. Through the noise of the growling sky and the breaking bowl, Lizzy slept fitfully, shivering sometimes, though the day was hot.

The younger orphans stayed with Rachel and Elizabeth again Friday night, helping out when they could. They were like a little group of neighbors who found themselves together during a terrible storm. Each of them drew some small comfort from the presence of the others. None could have said why.

No one saw Zebedee until late Saturday evening. He looked disheveled, as though he'd been in a fight. But no one wanted to ask him about it, not even Sarah. Zebedee entered silently and went over to Elizabeth's mat. Sensing his presence over her, she opened her eyes and smiled a weak smile cracking at the corners. He tried to smile back at her but couldn't seem to manage it.

After a moment, Zebedee lowered himself to the floor and pushed his long hair back from his face. Looking down between his knees, he said, in a low and raspy voice, "He's dead. They killed him."

"I know," whispered Lizzy.

Somehow, they had all known.

No one spoke.

There was a sniffle from Margaret and the sound of Sarah's heels bumping against the earthen wall as she swung her legs back and

forth from her perch on the window sill.
Otherwise, the room was still.

At last Rachel spoke. "His tomb?"

"A small cave near Golgotha," Zebedee
answered. "A lonely place. Not even a marker.
Just two Roman guards and a big rock rolled in
front of the entrance."

"To keep people from getting in?" Rachel
asked.

"Or Yeshua from getting out. Who
knows?"

"Are there any flowers?" Elizabeth asked
softly.

Zebedee shook his head.

Sarah banged her heels against the wall
angrily. "That's not fair!" she proclaimed. "Not
even flowers at his tomb."

"We will take him flowers," said Elizabeth,
her voice weak but firm.

Rachel heard the determination in that
voice. Never had her daughter looked so frail,
her eyes so hollow.

Yet Elizabeth's smiling assurance

persisted. Rachel noticed how the other children brightened at the prospect of gathering wild flowers.

Yes, Rachel thought, *in sorrowful times it is better to move, to move anywhere, than to stay still.*

Yet Rachel worried at the thought of Elizabeth attempting to climb the rough and rocky path to the burial place. Zebedee seemed to have read her thoughts as he spoke out in a commanding voice. "I will carry Elizabeth," he said.

Rachel thought: *He speaks like a man. The last few days have changed him. They've changed us all. I never met this teacher from Galilee, never even laid eyes on him. Yet he seems to have entered my life. Somehow we all are being led in a new direction. And we have no power to stop now. We can only lie upon the wind like dry leaves.*

"We'll carry her, too," chimed in Samuel and Simon.

There was nothing for Rachel but to

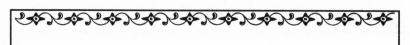

agree. With a quivering smile and a lump in her throat, she nodded.

Then she turned away so the children would not see her cry.

GATHER FLOWERS

The Lord took a seed, a little seed,
and laid it in the Earth.
He summoned the rain and sunshine
to give the flowers birth.

The lilies He made, with trumpets bold,
to greet the early morns,
The daisies with their secrets,
the roses with their thorns.

They say that the rain is heaven's tears;
God's blanket is the snow.
They say where God goes walking,
it's there the flowers grow.

And nothing a queen has ever worn,
no scepters kings may wield,
Is match for the precious flowers
that glorify the field.

So gather the flowers from vale and hill,
Go pick them wherever they lie.
A garland you'll string to scent my crib,
a wreath for when I die.

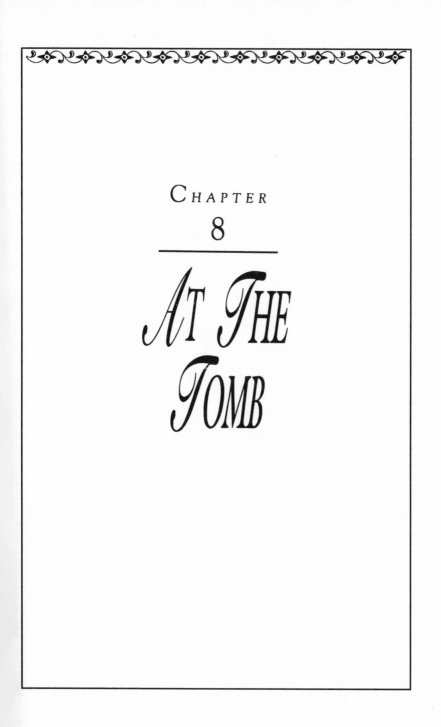

CHAPTER

8

AT THE
TOMB

*S*unday broke upon the hillsides of Jerusalem clear and fresh as a wave of cool water rushing across the desert. The earth seemed revitalized. There was a sound of wind in the distance, but the air hung still. The coolness came from something else. Perhaps it was the late dew lying on the grass, tickling bare feet as the children scrambled from cranny to nook gathering wild flowers.

Elizabeth seemed tickled as well, though her own feet happened to be dangling from a rock. She sat, immobilized by Rachel, watching the others gather bouquets of green, pink, yellow, orange, purple, and blue. Whenever Sarah, Rebecca, or Margaret collected an armful, the flowers would be dumped in Elizabeth's lap.

Looking on from a distance, Uncle Ezra shook his big head. "Yesterday, what? All gloom and doom, eh?" He nodded toward the orphans bending and plucking along the hillside. "And look at them today. Just because Elizabeth thought about picking flowers. You'd never imagine, hmm?"

Rachel was glad Elizabeth had thought to ask Uncle Ezra to join them. For the first time the old man seemed to understand that his little grandniece might never again run and play with her friends. He turned to Rachel and said softly, "She's like . . . well, like a light fading."

The words reminded Rachel of something Elizabeth had said to her the other day, speaking of her friend Lemuel. "Like a candle," she whispered to Uncle Ezra. "The candle stays burning, even when you take the spark away. But what happens when the candle is snuffed out? What happens then, Uncle?" Almost from the day Elizabeth had come to her, Rachel had known. She had known that someday, no matter how hard she pretended, this child would be taken from her.

They had held her close, all of them. They had sheltered her, protected her as they might shield a candle's flame from the currents of air. *And now*, she thought, *even as her own flame dies, each of ours will glow a little brighter because her spark touched us.*

Uncle Ezra turned and looked deep into Rachel's eyes, so full of surging emotion. Her smile was the smile that comes when love and sorrow mingle in the heart. The old man wrapped his arm around his niece, and she felt his rough gray beard quivering against her cheek. He was fighting back tears of his own.

Uncle Ezra is the only person, Rachel thought, *who knows all the wrongs I've done and yet still loves me.* But then a thought flew into her head, startling her. *No, he is not the only person. Elizabeth knows. Of course! She understands it all. Her love is great enough to forgive me everything—the fatherless home, the sickness, everything.*

"What say we, uh, get started, eh?" Uncle Ezra's voice woke her from her thoughts. "Mmm. Long walk. Sun not getting any lower, eh?" She smiled at him, then called to the children that it was time to leave for the burial place.

With arms full of flowers, they started up the hill. Lizzy rode horseback on Zebedee, who had woven flowers into her dark hair. As they trudged into the climbing sun they sang an old folk song about flowers.

"So gather the flowers from vale and hill," they sang, "Go pick them wherever they lie. A garland you'll string to scent my crib, a wreath for when I die." Since the tune was both sorrowful and spirited, it matched their mood perfectly.

AT THE TOMB

As they were walking, three veiled women passed them on the way down. The ladies seemed troubled, whispering anxiously among themselves. They carried towels and jars, and as they went by, Rachel caught the unmistakable scent of myrrh.

A few minutes later, Zebedee signaled a halt. He was standing next to a boulder as high as his shoulders. A few yards farther up the path was an opening in the hillside.

"This is it," said Zebedee, frowning. "But where are the soldiers? Yesterday there were soldiers. And this rock was pushed against the entrance up there. I didn't think we'd actually be able to get in. Now someone's rolled it down the hill."

"No way," said Simon and Samuel together. They were grunting, with their shoulders against the rock. "Take ten men to move this," said Samuel. "Twenty," said Simon.

Suddenly someone stepped from the darkness of the cave. It was a soldier, coming straight toward them.

Frightened, Rachel drew closer to Uncle Ezra, but he whispered, "It's all right. It's the same one. *Our* soldier."

"It is our soldier," said Elizabeth, smiling from her perch on Zebedee's shoulders.

The soldier who had visited their house seemed to be puzzling over a problem. He was deep in thought as he trudged slowly toward them, down the rocky path, leather scabbard slapping against leather leggings. Not until he was almost upon them did he take notice of Rachel, Uncle Ezra, and the children.

"Ah!" he said, stopping short. For a moment, the surprise seemed to push from his mind whatever he'd been puzzling over. Just for a moment his eyes went wide and his jaw slackened. Then, almost at once, the soldier's brow furrowed again and he rubbed his face with a coarse brown hand. He mumbled an absentminded "Ave," the Roman word for "hello," but his attention was on the enormous stone.

AT THE TOMB

Rachel recalled what Zebedee had said about soldiers guarding the tomb. *Was our friend one of the guards?* she wondered. And then she realized that she was actually thinking of a Roman, a soldier, as her friend. *We've all changed*, she told herself. *Something has happened to our world.*

The soldier spoke some words in Latin, still studying the rock. He felt around it with his hands, then put his shoulder to it. His legs and back stiffened. He pushed with all his might.

"He's trying to move it," Rachel gasped. "Get out of the way!"

Ezra shook his head, telling her not to worry. He was right. The soldier could not budge the boulder, no matter how hard he grimaced and strained, no matter how the sweat poured down his face and glistened along the curves of his bulging muscles. The old man placed his hand on the Roman's shoulder to calm him. The soldier's body shook with a spasm, his head collapsing against the stone.

He gasped for breath.

Margaret was peering cautiously around the rock, with Sarah tugging at her elbow. "Can't we go in now? Let's go in," the littlest orphan insisted.

Zebedee gently placed Elizabeth on the ground. "I'll make sure it's safe," he said. But Samuel and Simon had already disappeared into the cave, and the three girls were following close behind.

"Listen," said Rachel, gripping Ezra's sleeve. She was conscious of the wind, now suddenly louder, more insistent.

"Just, ah, the wind, you know. Whistling around that rock I suspect."

Yet the brown grass that fringed the cave was motionless. There was no wind. But then Rachel heard another sound, that of disappointed children.

"Hey."

"What's going on?"

"This place is empty."

"You brought us to the wrong cave, Zeb."

Sarah came running out in great agitation. "Can you believe it, Lizzy?" She stood with hands on her hips like a lady much put-upon. The wilting flowers and ferns drooped disappointedly down her leg. "There's no body in there. No body at all."

Margaret and the others followed Zebedee out. "You've got us lost, Zeb," she was shouting. "Admit it."

Zebedee looked around, a puzzled expression on his face. "No," he said. "I'm sure of it. This is Yeshua's tomb. Or so it was yesterday."

The sound of rushing wind seemed even louder now to Rachel. She looked to Uncle Ezra for guidance, but the old man was staring at the ground with knit brows, twisting and tugging at his beard. He seemed as puzzled as the Roman soldier was. The children continued clamoring, demanding at least a recognition from Zebedee that he, the oldest, had been wrong for once.

And then the noise abated as, one by one,

the children heard Elizabeth's voice coming to
them, faint and hollow. Automatically, they
looked to find her lying on the ground, but she
was not there. It was Uncle Ezra who spotted
her. "L-l-look," he stammered, pointing toward
the cave.

There, in the tomb's entrance, stood
Elizabeth, tall and erect, with a smile on her
face that told of wisdom as well as joy. She
seemed to glow, as though she were lit from
behind, by a light that had not been there
before, shining from the cave.

"Zeb is right," Elizabeth called out, her
voice hoarser but stronger. "This *was* Yeshua's
tomb, it really was. But no more, oh, no more."

"Lizzy," said Zebedee, "what . . ."

She interrupted him. "He is *alive!*"

"What, ah . . . Who . . ." spluttered
Uncle Ezra.

"What are you talking about?" demanded
Rachel. She was distracted by the sound of the
wind, which had taken on an almost musical
quality. The air was singing! But she brought

her attention back to Elizabeth and stepped toward the cave to help her. "Are you . . ."

"I'm fine now, Mother. Can't you see what's happened here? Can't you all see?" Lizzy searched them with her eyes. "Yeshua, the teacher. He's risen from the dead. _He's alive!_ That's why the tomb is empty."

Elizabeth became more animated with each breath, as though a new life was filling her very spirit. She stepped quickly to Zebedee, who was leaning against the big rock. "Zeb," she said, "you see it, don't you?"

Zebedee started to answer, but Elizabeth was already running to her friend Sarah. "It's a miracle," she exclaimed, "an honest-to-goodness miracle."

"Miracle!" Sarah echoed, as Elizabeth spun around in a pirouette of excitement.

"Uncle Ezra," she shouted, "remember how he raised that man?"

"Uh, Lazarus, yes." She was tugging at his striped robe. The girl was more worked up than he'd ever known her. He knew this was hard on her heart, and he did his best to calm her, holding her firmly by the shoulders.

"And how he fed the five thousand with Lemuel's bread and fish?" Lizzy skipped away from the old man, exuberant in her newfound energy. She ran to the weary soldier and hugged him, standing on tiptoe to plant a kiss on his cheek. The soldier stood dumbfounded.

"Remember how he made the deaf hear, Reba, and the blind see?"

"And our Lizzy *dance!*" cheered Margaret. "It is a miracle. It *is!*"

Rachel took her daughter's warm hands, hoping to still her, but little Sarah squeezed between them and went jumping up and down with Lizzy, dancing to the music of the wind. *If she's not cured*, Rachel thought, *at least she's forgotten how to be sick.*

"You feel it, don't you, Mother?" Elizabeth laughed as Sarah whirled her about. "Don't you believe?"

Rachel's eyes welled with tears, and she could only nod her agreement. Uncle Ezra suggested that it might be well for Lizzy to sit for a moment, but she replied, "No. We must take the flowers into the tomb."

"But, there's no, ah . . ."

"Just the same, we'll take them in." Elizabeth had an armload of flowers, and the other children were picking some up from where they had fallen on the ground. They could always depend on Lizzy to make them smile, in even the worst of times.

Rachel watched her daughter and the five orphans disappear into the darkness of the cave. The wind-music was dying.

"Lizzy . . . Lizzy!"

Sarah's voice, shrill and piercing, burst from within the cave and echoed against the boulder. Instinct seized the two men; the soldier and Uncle Ezra raced toward the tomb. But Rachel stiffened and turned away. Her own instincts, a mother's instincts, told her the meaning of Sarah's cry. The truth was in the cave, and she could not face the truth.

She listened as the wind-song faded and

ℳℐRACLE IN 𝒥ERUSALEM

fell away to silence. Never in her life had Rachel felt more alone. She waited for tears, but none came.

Behind her, though, she could hear the big soldier crying. She saw in her mind the tears mixed with perspiration on his face as he emerged into the sunlight, bearing the limp form of Elizabeth. The others would be following silently from the cave.

Rachel felt them all behind her, watching her, waiting for her to speak. She could not bear to face them yet. She must stand a while with her back to them, looking out over the rooftops of Jerusalem. One of those rooftops was her own, covering a house that would never again be as full as it once had been. *Has it all been a curse?* she wondered. *But if that's what it was, how could a curse bring me such joy, such wisdom? Why am I so much happier today for this curse on my life?*

"Mortua." The throaty voice of the Roman soldier broke the silence. Rachel recognized the Latin word for "dead."

Sarah, stifling her tears, shouted in an angry voice, "It's not fair."

"Not fair," the two brothers echoed.

At last Rachel turned and looked at her daughter, no longer her daughter. She moved toward the soldier slowly, deliberately, gathering strength. She stood before him and looked into his questioning blue eyes.

"Mortua," he said again.

Margaret, always quick to point out faults, said in a tearful, scornful voice. "There wasn't any miracle. No miracle at all."

Simon and Samuel spoke out together, agreeing with Margaret, as though their complaints could return Lizzy to life. Listening to them, Rachel knew at last what she must say.

"There *was* a miracle."

"Rachel . . ." Zebedee began, searching for an easy way to say it. "She's . . . she's . . ." He stammered like Uncle Ezra, a sob clutching at his throat. "She's *dead!*"

Rachel nodded and pulled downward on

the Roman soldier's arms, making him understand he was to lay Elizabeth's body on the hard-packed earth. Rachel knelt beside her daughter and brushed back the soft brown hair from the pale face. *Where has the life gone?* she wondered.

Rachel composed herself, then said, "You don't see it yet, do you? You don't see the miracle."

"I see that she's dead, that she's been taken away from us," answered Zebedee, bitterness like gall in his voice.

"But that's not the only thing," Rachel said. "The truly important thing is that she was *given* to us in the first place. The important thing is that we knew her at all. Won't you all try to see things the way Elizabeth begged us to see."

"Ah," Uncle Ezra began, "yes . . ."

"See with your *heart.* Zebedee, Margaret, Rebecca, all of you—see the miracle our Elizabeth was. See the teacher she was. Every moment she lived she taught us how to hope, how to love. And she taught me how to *believe*. Her life should teach us all how to open our hearts."

Uncle Ezra stood behind Rachel, stroking her own dark hair. "A teacher," he agreed, "yes, she was a teacher."

Rachel cradled Elizabeth's head in her lap and spoke so that only her uncle might hear. "They're all teachers, aren't they, Uncle Ezra? Every one of these children, and it's *we* who must keep learning from them."

She stroked the cool, lifeless cheek. All at once Rachel saw what she was being called to do, what Lizzy would want her to do. She must keep on hoping, keep on learning. She would open her home as well as her heart.

Rachel looked around at the brothers, Samuel and Simon, at stout, bossy Margaret, at shy Rebecca, and at thin, pugnacious Sarah. "I'll have an empty house now," she said. "Won't you all come and live with me? Make miracles for me?"

The orphans were too stunned to answer.

They were used to fending for themselves, accustomed to life on the streets of Jerusalem. At first they just looked at one another, not knowing what to say. At last little Sarah wriggled her way out of Uncle Ezra's grasp and ran to Rachel's side. First she bent to plant a kiss on Lizzy's forehead, then she threw her arms around Rachel, sniffling. Without speaking a word, she spoke for all of them.

Zebedee picked up Elizabeth's body. "We'll place it in the tomb," he said.

"With all the flowers," suggested Sarah.

The Roman soldier remained on the hillside as the Hebrews entered the cave, carrying the body of the child he had saved. He wiped his tear-dampened face with the back of his hand and slumped down against the boulder. *Strange*, he thought, *that a small, weak child could have such an effect.*

He recalled the words his commanding officer had spoken as the regiment disembarked from their ship at the Israeli port of Caesarea: "Rough, unfeeling animals, these Hebrews.

AT THE TOMB

Remember that, Marius, and you'll have no problem with them. You'll put in your time in this godforsaken place and be back in Rome before you ever know it. You'll forget you ever lived among them."

Somehow, the soldier thought, *that seems unlikely now.* He would never be able to forget these sad-sweet children and the pretty woman, frightened of him as a rabbit of a fox. Certainly he would never forget the man on the cross, never forget that look in his eyes as Marius touched the bleeding lips with a water-soaked cloth. There was a power in those eyes Marius never had felt before, not even in all the generals of Rome.

He picked up a flower dropped by one of the children and, without knowing why, began to examine it. Somehow the flower seemed to have life in it still, though it was no longer connected to its roots.

He looked toward the city of Jerusalem and sighed. He felt a wave of homesickness. How long could such a strong-willed people be held captive by a power so far away?

There was much the Roman did not understand. He would have to think things over.

ACKNOWLEDGMENTS

There are many good people without whose help this book might never have come about. First there is the author's wife, Joann, whose magical talents contributed in every phase, from conception to proofreading. There is his daughter, Beth, who inspired this book more than she will ever know. There are also friends who contributed in many ways: Jay Hobbs, Gary William Friedman, Kitty and George Greenberg, Sandy Weingart, and Sally McMillan.

ABOUT THE AUTHOR

Ross Paul Yockey is an Emmy award-winning writer/producer/director, a veteran of twenty-five years in journalism, television production and advertising. Among his seven previous books are *Zubin: The Zubin Mehta Story* and *Andre Previn, a Biography*, co-authored with Martin Bookspan, *New Orleans Scrapbook* and *A Century of Quality*. He has written a number of works for the stage, including three musical plays for children. He is founder of Plantain Publishing, a creative consulting company that produces educational, marketing, and management communications for business and industry.

A native of New Orleans and a former New Yorker, he lives in Charlotte, North Carolina, with his wife, Joann, and their daughter, Beth.